Peter's Railway
Holiday at Lunan Bay

by
Christopher Vine

The watercolour illustrations are by John Wardle

Published by
Christopher Vine 2014

Printed by The Amadeus Press

ISBN 978-1-9088970-46

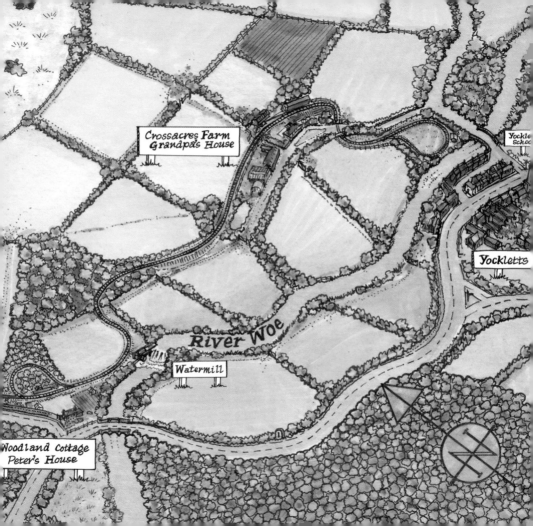

Crossacres Farm
Grandpa's House

Yockle
Schoo

Yockletts

River Woe

Watermill

Woodland Cottage
Peter's House

The Peter's Railway Series

Peter and Grandpa have built a miniature steam railway across Grandpa's farm. Originally it just ran between their houses, but now it links two villages and even takes the children to school.

They have had many adventures on the line, but this one takes place on a family holiday in Scotland.

The train crash which they investigate really happened and you can go and visit the site to see exactly what they saw. You might even find some more rivets under the bridge...

The Ordnance Survey grid reference for the point of collision is NO 685 519. Just don't trespass on railway property, it is dangerous!

Holiday at Lunan Bay

Peter, Kitty and Harry were on holiday in Scotland. The whole family were staying in a small hotel at Lunan Bay, a beautiful, long, sandy beach.

The first day found them by the sea having an enormous picnic. While the grown-ups were fixing up the food, the children were exploring the gigantic sand dunes.

They scrambled to the top of one and were enjoying the view when Harry had an idea. He did a roly-poly from the top! He tumbled over and over, in a tangled blur of arms and legs, laughing and screaming all the way down.

Soon everyone (except Grandma and Grandpa) was trying it.

After lunch, Grandpa climbed one of the dunes with the children.

From the top they could see a ruined castle (to be explored another day), miles of blue sea, white sand, and an attractive railway bridge.

"Let's go and have a better look at the bridge," suggested Grandpa. "We might even see a train going over it."

Scrambling across the dunes, they found the bridge carried the railway line over a deep gorge. At the bottom was a small stream which ran across the beach.

Whilst waiting for a train to rumble over, it was Peter's turn for a good idea.

"Why don't we build a dam on the beach and see how deep we can make the stream?" he suggested.

Back down by the sea, they found a good place to build their dam. Piling up sand and stones, Peter and Grandpa stopped the flow of water and held it back. A large pool started to form.

As the water flowed in, the pool got deeper and deeper. Soon they had to put more sand on top of the dam to stop the water going over the top.

Then the water went around the ends and started to wash the dam away. "We need more sand!" shouted Peter, digging frantically.

Kitty and Harry were busy too, making a sandcastle. They were building upstream of the dam so it would be surrounded by water to form a moat.

They had heaped up a large mound of sand to make an island, and now they were working on the walls and turrets.

It was a proper family day at the seaside.

That evening, back at the hotel, Grandpa was at the computer, printing out a document from the internet. "Look what I've just discovered," he exclaimed, waving some sheets of paper.

"I knew I'd read something about the railway at Lunan Bay," he grinned, "but I couldn't remember what it was.

"In 1958 there was a train crash here. No-one was hurt, but it must have been a spectacular smash. You won't believe the silly mistake that the crew of the first train made!

"I've printed out a map and the official accident report. Shall we go exploring tomorrow and see if we can find the exact spot where it happened?"

"Yes! Fantastic! A railway adventure!" the children shouted.

Tomorrow's fun was instantly fixed.

MINISTRY OF TRANSPORT AND CIVIL AVIATION

RAILWAY ACCIDENTS

REPORT ON THE COLLISION
which occurred on
2nd September 1958
near
LUNAN BAY
in the
SCOTTISH REGION
BRITISH RAILWAYS

LONDON HER MAJESTY'S STATIONERY OFFICE
1959
ONE SHILLING NET

At breakfast the next day, Peter, Harry and Kitty were looking at the map with Grandpa.

He was showing them where the accident had happened, but he was careful not to tell them too much about it. That would spoil the fun of telling them the story when they were standing at the site of the crash.

The map showed the line running from Dundee to Montrose, up the east coast of Scotland.

"The train which caused the crash was running north from Dundee," said Grandpa, pointing at the map. "The trouble started at Inverkeilor, a few miles south of here. But the collision happened some time later, just before Lunan Bay station.

"If we walk to the road bridge by the old station," suggested Grandpa, "we can explore from there."

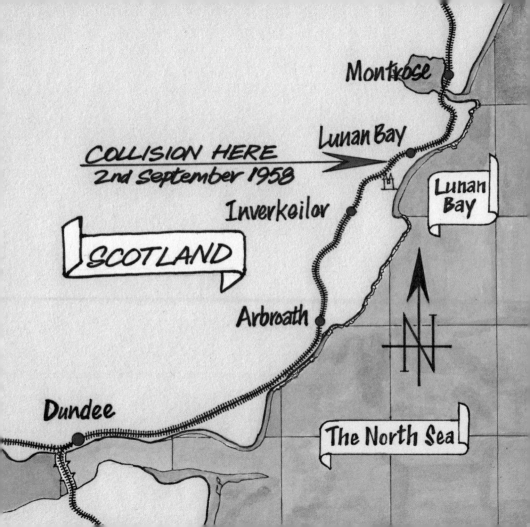

Fuelled by a huge breakfast, they walked up the road towards the old Lunan Bay station. They stopped on the bridge which crossed over the line.

Looking south, towards Inverkeilor, they could see another bridge. The railway could be seen under this bridge, before it curved away out of sight.

"The crash happened just down there," Grandpa pointed, "about 150 metres beyond that bridge, just out of sight around the bend.

"It was the bridge and the curve in the track which first led the men into making their crazy mistake," he explained.

"Once they had the wrong idea in their heads, they made everything else fit in with what they *thought* had happened. It was lucky no-one was killed, or even hurt."

Looking south, the bridge hides the view of the line beyond.

"On the 2nd of September 1958," began Grandpa, "at 7.09 in the morning, a passenger train left Edinburgh to run to Aberdeen. It was being hauled by a fast and powerful locomotive, one of the old London & North Eastern Railway's V2 class.

"To save running a separate goods train, they had hitched some goods wagons onto the back of the passenger carriages.

"There were eight passenger coaches, then a large and modern bogie wagon, followed by two old 4-wheeled fruit vans at the very end.

"These last two fruit vans were short vehicles and were not allowed to travel at speeds of more than 60 miles an hour. This meant that the whole train was restricted to 60 miles an hour."

"The maximum speed allowed on the line was 75 miles an hour, so it was important that the driver was informed of the speed restriction on his train because of the two old wagons at the rear.

"Well, the driver had been told and everything was fine to start with. However, at Dundee, a new driver and guard took over the train, but no-one told driver McRobb about the old wagons at the back and their speed limit.

"The seeds of disaster had been sown!" whispered Grandpa dramatically. "They were late and, to catch up, McRobb was going like the clappers. He was probably going at 75 miles an hour, if not more!

"Just past Inverkeilor station, the rear fruit van came off the track, but stayed attached to the train. It was dragged along like that for about 2 miles, bouncing on the sleepers and ballast stones."

"Nobody on the train noticed the derailed rear fruit van. The guard was in the middle of the train and the driver, at the front, could not possibly feel a bit of bumping at the back of such a long train. He carried on at full speed.

"Then," explained Grandpa, "the action moves on to a little bridge over a river and road. It's just out of sight from us, beyond that curve.

"It was there that the fruit van struck a part of the bridge and was thrown into the air. The coupling chain was wrenched off and the old van finally stopped after 100 metres, off the rails and blocking the track.

"When the fruit van became detached, it broke the vacuum brake pipe which runs the full length of the train. As the rubber connecting pipe was torn off, air immediately rushed in and the train's brakes all went on really hard."

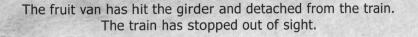

The fruit van has hit the girder and detached from the train.
The train has stopped out of sight.

Grandpa explained that the vacuum brake pipe ran the whole length of the train, with rubber connecting pipes between each of the wagons or carriages. This means that the brakes all along the train can be controlled from the driver's cab.

Normally, when the train is running, the pump on the engine would have sucked all the air out of the pipe to create a vacuum, and this would hold the brakes off. To apply the brakes, the driver pulls the brake lever in his cab which opens a valve, allowing air into the brake pipe.

Because this pipe runs the full length of the train, all the brakes are applied together.

But there's a special safety feature in the system: If the train splits in two, the brake pipe will be broken and air rushes in, putting the brakes on automatically. The brakes are applied on every vehicle to bring the train to a safe stop. It's called a fail-safe system.

Automatic Vacuum Brakes

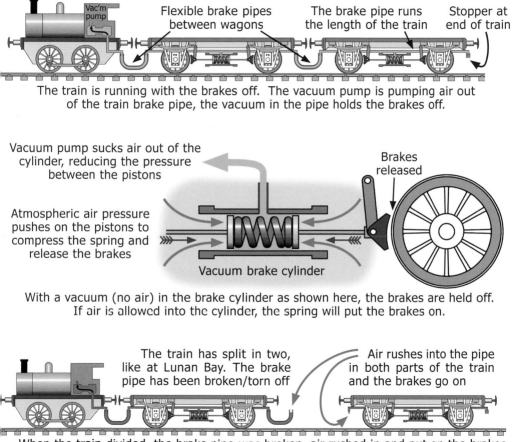

Vac'm pump

Flexible brake pipes between wagons

The brake pipe runs the length of the train

Stopper at end of train

The train is running with the brakes off. The vacuum pump is pumping air out of the train brake pipe, the vacuum in the pipe holds the brakes off.

Vacuum pump sucks air out of the cylinder, reducing the pressure between the pistons

Brakes released

Atmospheric air pressure pushes on the pistons to compress the spring and release the brakes

Vacuum brake cylinder

With a vacuum (no air) in the brake cylinder as shown here, the brakes are held off. If air is allowed into the cylinder, the spring will put the brakes on.

The train has split in two, like at Lunan Bay. The brake pipe has been broken/torn off

Air rushes into the pipe in both parts of the train and the brakes go on

When the train divided, the brake pipe was broken, air rushed in and put on the brakes.

"The first the driver knew of the problem," continued Grandpa, "was when he felt the brakes going on. The train came to a halt with its last wagon about 180 metres this side of that bridge down there. I think the engine must have stopped almost exactly under our feet, at this bridge here.

"Driver McRobb sent his fireman and guard to investigate why the brakes had gone on.

"Walking to the back of the train they saw the broken brake pipe and immediately jumped to the conclusion that this had caused the problem: The pipe had broken, air had leaked in and put the brakes on. Simple.

"They had seen the pipe was broken and they did think it was very odd. But," smiled Grandpa, "it was what they *didn't* see which was so important!"

"They did not see the detached fruit van, blocking the track, because it was beyond the bridge and out of sight round the curve in the line.

"They didn't notice that there was no red lamp at the back of their train - it was still on the back of the detached fruit van. Finally, they didn't notice that the rear of their train now had two coupling chains: its own and one wrenched from the fruit van.

"They jumped to the crazy conclusion that the brake pipe had just broken by itself! Sort of fallen to pieces...

"So, with no further thought, they decided to fix the pipe by using the stopper-plug on the brake pipe on the back of the next wagon.

"Now, with the end of the pipe plugged up, the locomotive could recreate the vacuum and the driver would be able to release the brakes and restart the train."

The fruit van is out of sight, around the bend.

"Driver McRobb was keen to get going again, to catch up lost time. So as soon as his fireman reappeared and told him what had happened, he set off. They called out to the Lunan Bay signalman as they passed, and told him what had happened.

"McRobb did think it was peculiar that the pipe had just broken, but he did no more about it.

"Passing the next signal box at Usan, there was one last chance to avoid a crash. The signalman should have noticed there was no red light at the back of the train. It was a vital part of his job and would have warned him that a wagon had been left behind.

"However, he was too busy looking at the mysterious broken pipe which he had been told about on the telephone by the signalman from Lunan Bay!

"Without any further thought, he sent the 'Line Clear' message back to the signal box at Inverkeilor. Another train could now follow up the line…"

"Meanwhile, just two minutes later, our train arrived at Montrose. Guard Kessack went back to see about replacing the broken brake pipe.

"Looking at the back of the train, he suddenly noticed the missing lamp and extra coupling chain. He nearly fainted with shock as he realised his awful blunder. They had lost a wagon and it must be blocking the line!

"He ran to the signal box. 'Obstruction! Danger!' he shouted, waving frantically. 'The line's blocked!'

"There was uproar at Montrose. Bell signals, telephone calls and lots of shouting.

"They were desperately trying to get all the signals along the line placed at danger, to stop the following train.

"But it was too late."

"A north-bound express train had already passed clear signals at Inverkeilor and was now bearing down on the old fruit van, stranded across the line.

"The driver, Mr Fraser, was working the engine hard as they climbed the steep hill towards Lunan Bay. The fireman, Mr Morrison, was shovelling coal on the fire, to keep up the steam pressure.

"Looking up from his fire, Morrison suddenly saw the fruit van, off the rails, about 100 metres in front of them. It was just coming into view round the curve.

"He shouted at Fraser, who slammed on the brakes and was starting to put the engine into reverse gear.

"It wasn't their fault, but they were much too close to stop."

"The express engine ploughed into the fruit van.

"The van was completely wrecked, the front of the engine was damaged and about 80 metres of the track was ruined. It was a miracle that no-one was hurt."

"It must have been a spectacular mess!" grinned Peter, as they all imagined the scene.

"Let's see if we can find the exact spot where it happened," Grandpa suggested. "We mustn't go onto railway property, but we can stand in the field beside it."

The children led the way, with Grandpa following. Across one field, through a gate and half-way across another, they found themselves standing where the crash had happened, nearly 60 years ago.

"It's strange," said Peter. "After all that drama and destruction, there's no evidence of it at all. It's just a peaceful field and railway. Surely there should be something to show what happened."

"Let's go and look at that bridge," said Grandpa, pointing down the line. "The fruit van smashed into one of its girders; maybe some damage will still be visible."

Five minutes later, they were standing under the bridge and peering up at the steel girders.

"Look!" pointed Peter. "Everything is riveted together except that part there."

Grandpa looked and it was quite obvious, they were looking at the girder which had been damaged in 1958. It had been repaired by welding in a new section. The evidence was still there, right in front of them. It made the whole story seem very real.

While Peter and Grandpa were still looking at the girders, Kitty and Harry were exploring the river bank below the bridge. "Look what I've found!" shouted Harry excitedly. "What is it?!"

He was holding something rusty in his hand.

"It's a rivet," exclaimed Grandpa. "You've found one of the rivets from when they repaired the bridge. You have picked up a piece of history!"

Of course they all started hunting for more rivets and soon their pockets were bulging. They were perfect souvenirs from a grand day of railway archaeology and adventure!

"If you think about the crash," said Peter while they were walking back to the hotel, "the strange thing is that the fireman and guard never realised that the rear van had separated from the rest of the train. It was so obvious and yet they missed it."

"It is strange," agreed Grandpa, "but it happens quite often. People can easily jump to the wrong conclusion. Then they make everything else they see fit in with what they *think* is happening.

"There was a bad boiler explosion at Cardiff, in 1909," Grandpa remembered. "The fitters had made a mistake when they rebuilt the safety valves on the boiler, so that they were locked shut and could not let steam escape when the pressure became too high.

"Driver Lewis saw the pressure gauge showing 200 psi (pounds per square inch), which was already well above the boiler's safe working pressure. The safety valves weren't lifting to release the excess steam, so he jumped to the disastrous conclusion that the pressure gauge was not reading correctly.

"There were lots of clues that the pressure was too high," added Grandpa, "but the driver kept ignoring them, still believing the pressure gauge was wrong."

How high was the pressure ?
The needle was pressed against the pin
so it was at least 200 pounds per square inch (psi).
The red line shows the maximum allowed pressure was 160 psi.
Steam pressure might have been 300 or 400 psi, no-one will ever know.
Both water gauge glasses had broken, a clear sign that the pressure
was dangerously high. But the men still believed the pressure gauge was wrong.
In fact the pressure gauge was reading correctly, warning of danger.

"The boiler finally exploded with such tremendous force that it completely destroyed the locomotive and landed 40 metres away. It was a serious accident."

Later that evening, during dinner, the children were talking non-stop about train crashes, broken brake pipes, pressure gauges and boiler explosions.

Finally Grandma interrupted them. "This is a seaside holiday," she gently reminded. "Tomorrow, why don't you do normal beach activities, like swimming in the sea and flying kites?"

"Oh yes," the children agreed. "Flying kites would be great. And Grandpa can tell us all about aerodynamics!"

Grandma and Mum sighed and raised their eyes upwards. What a family!

The End.

Why Peter's Railway?

Since a very small boy, Chris has always loved everything mechanical, especially steam engines. The first workshop was in his bedroom where he made an electric go-kart aged 8, followed by a mini-bike powered by the engine from a petrol lawn mower.

He spent many holidays on a friend's farm where there was a miniature railway across a field and so started a love of making model steam locomotives. The latest is Bongo, 8 feet long and the inspiration for Fiery Fox in the books.

Chris wanted to share his love and knowledge of railways and engineering: Peter's Railway is the result.

Books for children who love trains and engineering

Story

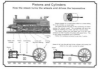
Technical

History

Adventure

The hardback books

The five hardback books tell the charming story of Peter and his Grandpa building and running their steam railway across the farm. At the ends of chapters are special how-it-works pages with simple (but accurate) explanations of what has been happening in the story. In addition, Grandpa tells some wonderful stories from the old days on the railways. Age range 6 - 12 years approx.

A new steam railway is born.

Points, turntables and Peter drives Fiery Fox.

The line is extended and The Great Railway Race.

They build a watermill to power the farm.

Peter helps save the world and makes lots of money!

Activity book with puzzles and colouring. Paperback.

Hardback, 96 pages 17 x 24 cm with 30 watercolour pictures by John Wardle and 14 pages of clearly explained technical drawings. £11.99

Paperback books

A series of Peter's Railway in a smaller format. While the original books each contain several story or adventure threads, separate technical pages and Grandpa's tales, the small books concentrate on one aspect; an adventure, a tale from the old railways or a technical book.

"Little" Peter's Railway are gentle stories for younger children.

Grandpa entertains the children and mayhem follows...

A bed-time story with a twist...

Peter saves Christmas.

Grandpa answers a tricky question.

A true story about an unlucky locomotive.

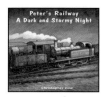

A dramatic true story from the old days.

A cab-ride in a modern train and a tale of a near disaster.

Our two heroes make a new engine.